Syrian Folktales

by Muna Imady

To my mother and father with all my love.

For information, contact
MSI Press
1760-F Airline Highway, #203
Hollister, CA 95023

Cover and maps designed by Sammy Zarka

Library of Congress Control Number 2011944900

ISBN: 9781933455099

Table of Contents

Syrian Folktales

Kan ya ma kan are magic words that carry me back into my Tete's little red bedroom forty years ago. I see myself sitting on her bed listening to her stories on a very cold winter night. The lit *soba* in the corner of the room casts shadows on the walls. The shadows dance and transform themselves into the characters created by Tete. I reach my hands towards them, but they slip away. Tete laughs and takes out a bag of pistachios from under her pillow and fills my little hands with them.

Most of the stories I remember Tete telling me were told to me in the evenings. I wonder... was it a matter of convenience, or did Tete believe that darkness was the best time to tell stories?

Actually, in the old days, Arabs felt that telling stories in daylight was bad luck. Daytime was naturally for serious and domestic housework, while night was the time for stories of make-believe.

In the Euphrates region, people still say: "*Illi yekhoref fee an-nahar, beseer heemar*" which means: "Whoever tells stories in the daytime turns into a donkey."

To this day, folktales still fascinate me. I pity my children when I see them taken by the ever-lasting TV programmes and computer games that have kidnapped them from the fascinating mystical world I enjoyed when I was their age.

So many things have changed since I was a little girl. Computer games, the internet, mobile phones and satellite channels all have invaded the hearts and the minds of Syrian children of the twenty-first century. This technology not only affects the children but their mothers. I was struck by the fact that even women my age had to ask their mothers to get me a folktale from their province.

As Western folktales have their evil witches and dragons, many Syrian folktales also have evil and hideous supernatural beings. There are the *ghouleh* which is female and something like a witch and the *afreet*, which is male. Both are considered a kind of jinn and have magical powers.

In this book, in addition to the folktales, I have included recipes from all the Syrian provinces, riddles, sayings and street peddler songs to give the reader a broad picture of Syrian folklore.

I hope this modest attempt to collect and preserve the ever-dying folklore in Syria will be followed by a comprehensive work of experts in this field.

A Brief Overview of Syria

The Syrian Arab Republic occupies an area of 185000 square km. and has a population of more than 18 million. It borders Turkey to the north, Iraq to the east, Jordan and Palestine to the south and Lebanon and the Mediterranean to the west. Syria also lies along major trade routes linking Africa, Asia and Europe.

Since the dawn of civilization, Syria has been a meeting place and a crossroads, where different people, cultures and world empires met. Syrian soil has witnessed the oldest civilizations on the globe dating back to the fourth millennium B.C., including Mari, Ebla and Ugarit where one the world's first alphabets was discovered.

Syria's chief agricultural products are: cotton, wheat, barley, different fruits and vegetables, meat, milk and milk products. Important industrial products include: textiles, fertilizer, petroleum products, cement, glass, processed foods, marble, petroleum and phosphates.

The Syrian Arab Republic consists of fourteen administrative units known as governorates *(Muhafazat)*. Every governorate in Syria has its own folklore traditions passed down from generation to generation. These include stories, sayings, riddles, recipes for tasty local dishes and embroidery patterns and the cut of traditional dresses. I feel it is important to record these tales, traditions, peddlers' chants and recipes before they are completely forgotten. It would be a sad loss if Syria forgets its rich oral traditions and regional dishes. As I take you through Syria and its different governorates, I hope what I present here will charm you and give you a small idea of the variety of Syrian traditional culture.

The *Muhafaza* of Damascus

Damascus is not only the capital of Syria, but is also one of the fourteen governorates of the country. In addition, it is world famous for being one of the oldest continuously inhabited cities in the world. Many civilizations have left their mark on it over the centuries: Aramaen, Greek, Roman, Byzantine and Arab. Yet it co-existed with them, preserving their influence and monuments.

The city of Damascus owes everything to the Barada for this river waters the gardens, fields and orchards around the city, the oasis from which the city gets much of its food.

Damascus is distinguished for its old and modern aspects, where archaeological remains hundreds of years old and up-to-date buildings stand together side by side. Some of the most important historical monuments are the Umayyad Mosque, the Roman arches of the Temple of Jupiter, the Azem Palace, Khan Assad Pasha, the Citadel and the Chapel of St. Ananias.

A Damascene Folktale: The Three Spinners

Once upon a time there lived three sisters who were very poor. Their father and mother had died, leaving them only the little house they lived in. To earn money, they spun wool into yarn and then sold it in the market.

One day, the oldest sister said, "How I wish I could eat a roasted sheep stuffed with spicy rice and almonds!"

The middle sister closed her eyes and drew a long breath and said, "How lovely the stuffed roasted sheep would taste with green onions!"

The younger sister added enthusiastically, "It would taste even better with some red radishes!"

The three sisters laughed and decided to save their money to buy a sheep and cook it stuffed with spicy rice and almonds.

Time passed, the three sisters worked hard spinning the yarn into thread and dreaming of their roasted stuffed sheep.

As they spun they sang joyfully:

How very tasty and how very nice
Is roasted sheep stuffed with almonds and rice!
Green onions and radishes would also be nice
With the sheep stuffed with almonds and spicy rice!

Finally, the three sisters saved enough money to fulfill their dream. They went down to the market, bought a sheep and cooked it with rice and almonds. They set the roasted sheep on a large tray decorated with almonds and pistachios. Then the three sisters happily sat down to eat, but the older sister suddenly called out, "Oh my God, we have forgotten to get green onions!"

Then the youngest sister said, "We have forgotten to get red radishes!"

The three sisters ran out of their house towards the nearby fields. They were in such a rush that they forgot to close the door of their house. As they ran they sang joyfully:

How very tasty and how very nice
Is roasted sheep stuffed with almonds and rice!
Green onions and radishes would also be nice
With the sheep stuffed with almonds and spicy rice!

As they ran through their neighborhood towards the fields, the garbage man saw them. He patiently waited for them to disappear, then slipped into their house and carried out the tray of roasted sheep to his poor old mother. They both hadn't tasted meat for such a long time that they ate everything on the tray.

When the three sisters reached their house, they couldn't believe their bad luck. They cried and screamed and hit each other with the green onions and red radishes. Their sorrow and grief was so deep that they died shortly after their roasted stuffed sheep had been stolen.

Riddle

Oh, clattering bowl
Floating in the sea
Copper is its skin
Pearls are within.
What is it? Answer: a pomegranate

Lullaby

This old lullaby reflects the sorrows and sadness of mothers in general. Different generations added new touches according to their own experiences. It was well-known at the beginning of the 20th century.

Ola ya olani
The Caravan of Hajj has gone
And I'm left all alone!
The pilgrim has returned home
Oh God, don't forget me
Give me of your generosity
Ola ya olani
Sleep, my daughter, sleep
I'll kill a dove for you
Oh dove, don't believe it
I'm only joking so my daughter will sleep.
Sleep. my daughter, sleep
The eye of Allah never sleeps.
How the hearts of people
Have hardened, my daughter,
Their hearts haven't softened!
Stop opening up wounds.
Sleep, my daughter, sleep

I hope you will never be troubled.
Your eyes, my daughter,
Have shut with delight.
Oh yes, my daughter,
Ola, ya olani

A Damascene Recipe for *Kibbeh*

A long time ago the daily life of Damascene house-wives revolved around the preparation of *kibbeh*. They pounded the meat and cracked wheat (*burghol*) in a metal mortar with a heavy metal pestle and then shaped the shells by hand. Today, an electric food processor that combines the meat and *burghol* has relieved women of the most difficult part of the preparation of *kibbeh*.

Kibbeh Filling – Ingredients:

1 pound of ground lamb.
1 medium onion finely chopped.
4 tablespoons of butter.
1/2 a teaspoon of cinnamon.
1/2 a teaspoon of pepper.
1/2 a teaspoon of salt
1/2 a cup of pine nuts.

Method:
- Fry onions in oil until golden.
- Add meat and pine nuts to the onions, and cook adding a few tablespoons of water to soften the meat.
- Add cinnamon, pepper and salt.

Kibbeh Shell – Ingredients:
   1 pound of ground lamb.
   1 large onion.
   2 cups of fine *burghol*.
   1/2 a teaspoon of salt.
   1/2 a teaspoon of pepper.
   Oil to fry the *kibbeh*.

Method:
- Rinse *burghol* in a pan of water then drain the water in a strainer and squeeze out all moisture.
- Add the ground meat, onions, salt and pepper to the *burghol*.
- Grind all ingredients together in a food processor and then knead well by hand until smooth and moist.
- Wet your hand with cold water and take a small lump of *kibbeh* mixture. Hold it in your left hand and make a hole with your finger then widen the hole and flatten the walls until a hollow oval shape is formed.
- Fill the shell with the filling.
- Close by sticking the edges together.
- Fry the *kibbeh* in oil.

Hadith – A saying of the Prophet (pbuh)

Wahshi bin Harb relates that some of the companions of the Holy Prophet (pbuh) said to him: "O Messenger of Allah, we eat but don't get satisfied." He said: "Perhaps you are eating alone." They said:"Yes, oh Messenger of Allah, that is true." He told them: "Eat together and invoke the name of Allah before eating and then the food will be blessed for you."

Reported by Abu Daud

("pbuh" means "peace be upon him" - Muslims add this after mentioning the Prophet)

Muna Imady

The *Muhafaza* of Rural Damascus

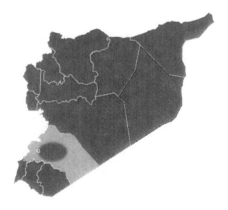

This *muhafaza* includes the rural areas surrounding the city of Damascus and occupies an area of 17654 square km. Most of the population of this *muhafaza* work in agriculture while some have industrial or service occupations. It includes eight sections and twenty one areas, but I have included only Mouadamieh and the Ghouta.

Mouadamieh

Mouadamieh lies in a wide plain surrounded by mountains, and used to be one of the most beautiful villages of the Ghouta before large cement buildings sprouted there. Nevertheless, doctors still recommend its dry air for their patients that have diseases of the chest.

A Folktale from Mouadamieh:
"*Nuss-insais*" or "Tiny"

Once upon a time, there was a man who had three wives but no children to fill his life with happiness. One day, while the man was sitting at the doorstep, a street peddler passed by calling: "Mountain apples for pregnancy!"

The man rushed towards the peddler and bought three apples. He called his three wives and gave them each an apple.

His first and second wives ate their apples, while his third wife just ate half of it and left it on the window sill.

Later on, a donkey passed by and ate it. Soon the three wives were pregnant and in a matter of months they had three healthy sons. The first and the second wife named their sons Mohammed and Hassan. The son of the third wife was so small that they called him Nuss-insais, or Tiny.

When the three boys grew up, their father asked what they wanted him to buy them.

"We each want a horse and a gun!" said Mohammed and Hassan.

"What about you, Nuss-insais, don't you wish for something?"

"O, yes," answered Nuss-insais, "I want a mule and a long stick!"

His two brothers laughed at Nuss-insais's wish and made fun of him. Ever since Nuss-insais was a child; his brothers had always teased him about his small size.

"Someday I will show them all what I can do!" said Nuss-insais as he shook his head determinedly.

One day, the three boys went out hunting. Nuss-insais caught many birds with his long stick, while his two brothers couldn't kill a single bird with their guns.

On their way back home they got lost in the desert. Suddenly they saw an old ugly woman standing at the foot of a hill.

The old woman smiled at them and said: "I'm your old Auntie… don't you remember me?"

"We have no Auntie" said the three boys. "Our father has no sisters!"

"What!" croaked the old woman "Your hard-hearted father didn't tell you about me! Come in my dear nephews and I'll feed you something good to eat!"

The three boys went into the cave and were properly fed. Then the old woman asked them: "What do your horses and mule drink?"

"Milk!" said Mohammed and Hassan.

"Water!" said Nuss-insais.

Mohammed and Hassan were touched by the old woman's special treatment and said to each other, "Only a true aunt would receive us so warmly!" But Nuss-insais shook his head and said: "Wouldn't we have heard of her from our father?"

As night fell, the boys were led to a big bedroom to spend the night. Somehow Nuss-insais couldn't go to sleep; he kept hearing strange loud howling from a distance.

Nuss-insais crept outside the room and peeked at his aunt. To his horror, his so-called aunt was a terrifying *ghouleh* (a kind of a witch). Her hair was wild and her eyes were blazing red.

At dawn, when the *ghouleh* went out to the well, Nuss-insais woke up his brothers and told them what he had seen. At once they jumped on their horses and ran away.

When the *ghouleh* finally came back, she found their room abandoned. She fell into a rage, and howled so loud that the walls of the cave rang. Then she ran outside and said out loud:

"O my milk, steam and bubble

Hold up their horses on the border"

The horses of both Mohammed and Hassan stopped at once. However, Nuss-insais's mule hadn't drunk milk and it kept on running. The two brothers jumped off their horses and ran after Nuss-insais.

When the three brothers finally reached home, they told their father about their adventure.

"I want a big wooden trunk!" said Nuss-insais.

"What on earth are you going to do with a trunk?" asked his father.

"I want to get rid of the *ghouleh* for once and for all!" said Nuss-insais.

When Nuss-insais got his trunk, he filled it with colorful costume jewelry, shiny glass beads and baubles and dressed himself up as a peddler. He put the big trunk on his mule and went off to find the *gouleh*.

When the *ghouleh* saw Nuss-insais she was very suspicious of him, but as soon as he opened up the trunk she was taken by the glittering things inside.

"You might find surprising things if you step inside the trunk." said Nuss-insais.

As soon as the *ghouleh* stepped inside, Nuss-insais closed the lid of the trunk and locked it. Then he carried the trunk back home.

"Hurry up and build up a big fire!" called out Nuss-insais. "This is our chance to get rid of the *ghouleh* and her wicked ways forever!"

People rushed out of their houses and piled up pieces of wood and built up a great fire then threw the wooden trunk in it and that was the end of the terrible *ghouleh*.

From that day on, no one ever again made fun of Nuss-insais for being so tiny.

Riddle

Four black men
Travelling on a stick
Go to and fro
When the wind does blow
What are they? Answer: eggplants

Four Recipes from Mouadamieh:

1. *Kibbeh Assaferi* or Bird *Kibbeh*

This kind of *kibbeh* is cooked by the wives of bird hunters in Mouadamieh. It has the same ingredients used in the Damascene *kibbeh* mentioned before, and follows the same steps, except that ground-up birds are added to the *kibbeh* shell ingredients.

Method:
- Pluck the birds and cut off their heads and legs.
- Rub with salt and pepper.

- Place the birds in a metal mortar and pound them until they form a solid mixture.
- Mix with the *kibbeh* shell ingredients and continue as in the *kibbeh* recipe for Damascus.

2. Stuffed Chicken Necks

Ingredients:
2 pounds of chicken necks.
1 stick of cinnamon.
1 bay leaf and a 2 cardamom pods.
a sprinkle of saffron.
3/4 of a teaspoon of black pepper.
3/4 of a teaspoon of cinnamon.
3 tablespoons of tomato paste.
1 pound of ground lamb.
1/2 a cup of half cooked chickpeas.
1 cup of rice.
2 Maggi cubes.

Method:
- Remove bones and meat from the chicken necks.
- Wash the neck skins and rub with salt and lemon inside and out.
- Sew up one side of each neck with needle and thread.
- Combine the rice, meat, spices and chick peas then stuff the chicken necks.
- Place the chicken meat and bones in a pan then add the stuffed necks.
- Add water, tomato paste, Maggi cubes, bay leaf and cardamom.
- Cook for an hour or until done.

3. Potato Pies

Basic dough – Ingredients:
  1 pound of flour.
  3/4 of a cup of oil
  1 tablespoon of salt.
  1 tablespoon of sugar.
  1 tablespoon of yeast.
  1 and 1/2 a cup of lukewarm water.

Method:
- Combine the ingredients, mix well and knead until smooth.
- Cover and let rest until dough rises.
- Cut into small balls. Then flatten with your hands and make small pies.

Filling – Ingredients:
  1 pound of ground beef.
  2 pounds of potatoes.
  1\3 cup of butter.
  1 large onion.
  salt and pepper to taste.

Method:
- Peel the potatoes and grate them.
- Add a pinch of salt to take away the moisture.
- Sauté beef in butter.
- Grate the onion and combine with the ingredients and squeeze out all moisture.
- Place the filling on the dough and arrange pies on an oiled baking tray and bake in oven (350) until done - maximum 15 minutes.

4. *Burghol* (cracked wheat) with Meat

Ingredients:

1 cup of washed and soaked rough *burghol.*
1/2 a pound of lamb cut into 1- inch cubes.
6 cups of water.
1 tablespoon of tomato paste.
1 teaspoon of salt.
1 cup of washed and soaked chick peas.
2 squeezed lemons.
2 cloves of mashed garlic.
fried bread.

Method:

- Cook the meat in the 6 cups of water.
- Add the *burghol,* chickpeas and salt until done.
- Add the tomato paste and cook 15 minutes on a low fire.
- Serve with lemon juice, mashed garlic and fried bread.

Hadith

Abu Hurairah says that the Holy Prophet (pbuh) never found fault with any food. If he liked it, he would eat it; if he disliked it, he would leave it.

Reported by Bukhari and Muslim

Hadith

Ibn Abbas relates that the Holy Prophet (pbuh) said: Do not drink water in one gulp like a camel, but take it in two or three sips. Invoke the name of Allah when you start drinking and praise him when you finish.

Reported by Al Tirmizi

The Ghouta

The word "Ghouta" literally means, "an orchard full of trees" and is the name for the fertile land which lies to the east and the west of the city Damascus. It is quenched by the Barada river and is filled with orchards of apple, apricot, olive and peach trees. Its inhabitants are mostly farmers who, in addition to cultivating orchards of fruit trees, also raise wheat, vegetables and walnuts.

A Folktale from the Ghouta: The Wicked Stepmother

Long ago, on the edge of the Ghouta, there lived a little girl called Fatima. Her mother had died when she was very young and left her with her loving father.

In a house nearby lived a woman who frequently visited them to take care of Fatima. One day the woman embraced Fatima and said, "I love you as if you were my own child. Ask your father to marry me and I promise you a very happy life."

When the father returned back from work, Fatima asked her father, "Why don't you marry our neighbor, father?"

"You are too young and I love you very much," said the father. "I'm afraid that she will mistreat you."

"Please," said Fatima. "She seems to be such a nice person. We can all live together as happily as can be."

"Stepmothers hate their husband's children," said her father.

"She is different from the other women you know," Fatima said. "She is a very loving woman."

In the end the father listened to the wishes of his daughter and married the neighbor.

Once the neighbor got married to Fatima's father, she changed from a kind neighbor into a cruel stepmother and turned Fatima's life into hell. She made Fatima do all the housework from morning to dusk.

Years passed and Fatima turned into a beautiful young lady. Unfortunately, the prettier Fatima became, the more jealous her stepmother was of her.

One day, the stepmother decided to get rid of Fatima for good. She called Fatima and said cheerfully, "I'm cooking a fine meal for you, but I need a sieve. I want you to go into the Ghouta and fetch me a sieve from the *ghouleh.*"

Fatima was terrified to go to the *ghouleh*, but was even more afraid to disobey her stepmother, so off she went. On her way to the *ghouleh*, Fatima met some farmers picking roses. At once, she joined the farmers and helped them. One of the old farmers was so pleased with her that he held up a red rose and said, "May Allah make your cheeks as red as this rose."

Later on as Fatima walked along, she met a horse giving birth. She rushed towards it and helped it deliver its foal. The horse was so touched by her kindness that it said, "May Allah make your hair as long as my mane."

At last, Fatima reached the *ghouleh's* cottage. Trembling with fear, Fatima knocked at the door. Suddenly, the door was thrown open and the *ghouleh* stood in front of Fatima. She peered at the girl suspiciously and asked, "What can I do for you, my dear?"

"I've come to ask for a sieve," Fatima said.

The *ghouleh* smiled fiendishly at her and said, "Come in my dear, you must be tired after your long walk through the Ghouta. You are most welcome and may dirty my cottage, break my door and even kick my cow!"

The *ghouleh* shuffled out of the cottage and Fatima did exactly the opposite of what the *ghouleh* asked her to do. She cleaned the house, oiled the rusty hinges of the door and fed the cow.

When the *ghouleh* returned, she asked Fatima to smash the windowpanes and slaughter the hens and then left the cottage again.

While she was gone, Fatima cleaned the windows and fed the hens. When the *ghouleh* returned again carrying a sieve, she was so happy and pleased with Fatima that she threw her in the well and said:

"Well, well, well...

Give Fatima what she deserves

For she has done so well."

And then Fatima climbed out of the well wearing a silk gown and a golden ring.

The *ghouleh* handed Fatima the sieve and thanked her for what she had done.

While Fatima was running back home, she somehow lost her new golden ring and it was later found by the King while he was out hunting with his men.

Holding up the ring with admiration, the King said, "I will not get married except to the owner of this ring!"

The King's mother visited every house in the kingdom to find the owner of the ring. Every young girl had to try the ring on her finger, but unfortunately it didn't fit anyone.

"Are you sure you knocked on every door in the kingdom?" the King asked his mother.

"Well… almost," answered the King's mother. "There's a small cottage at the edge of the Ghouta that I didn't visit."

"O please go and see if there is a young lady living there," said the King.

The King's mother reluctantly went to the cottage at the edge of the Ghouta and knocked on the door. The stepmother opened the door and when she heard the reason for the visit, she eagerly snatched the ring from the King's mother. She tried to force the ring on her finger, but with no luck. When it was Fatima's turn to try the ring on, it slipped on her finger and fit perfectly.

The King's mother took Fatima's hand and led her off to the palace, where she was married to the King.

The stepmother was now even more jealous of Fatima and decided to get revenge on her. She invited Fatima to the *hammam* (public bath) and offered to scrub her and comb her hair. As she was combing Fatima's hair, she poked a pin into her head.

"Ouch, that hurts!" cried out Fatima.

"I'm sorry," said her stepmother. "It must be this old comb I'm using."

But the stepmother slyly kept on poking pins into Fatima's head, until she suddenly turned into a bird and fluttered around the *hammam*.

When the King came back for his wife, the stepmother pointed at a bird standing next to the fountain of the *hammam* and said: "That's your wife!"

The King held the bird lovingly and patiently started to pull out the pins from its body. When the last pin was pulled out, Fatima was turned back into a beautiful woman again.

As soon as the King returned with Fatima to the palace, he ordered his men to arrest the stepmother and throw her in prison. With the stepmother behind bars, the King and Fatima lived together happily ever after.

Riddle

I'm big as a *kibbeh* globe
Dressed in a robe
What am I? Answer: an onion

Two Recipes from Urbeen in the East Ghouta:

1. *Tutnajeh*

This dish is cooked about three days before the wedding day to celebrate the happy occasion within the family circle.

Ingredients:
1/2 a cup dried fava beans, skinless soaked overnight.
1 cup lentils.
4 cups water to boil fava beans and lentils.
2 cups flour.
2 cups lukewarm water.
1/2 a teaspoon salt.
2 big onions, thinly sliced and fried in olive oil.
1/2 a cup *kishik.**

1 cup olive oil.
1 bunch of coriander.
1 loaf of Arabic bread cut into small squares and fried in olive oil.
1 squeezed lemon.

Method:
- Add drained fava beans and lentils to 4 cups of water. Cook until beans and lentils are tender. Then set aside.
- Mix 2 cups of flour with 2 cups of lukewarm water and 1/2 a teaspoon of salt.
- Knead the dough well and roll with a rolling pin. Then cut it into squares.

---

*Kishik is made from yogurt, ground wheat and spices. This mixture is allowed to ferment and dry for many days in the sun, then run through a sieve until it is a fine dry powder.

- Add 1/2 cup of kishik to the fava beans and lentils and cook stirring constantly until the kishik dissolves.
- Wash and cut the coriander and fry with olive oil
- Bring the pot to a boil and add the square pieces of dough, one by one, to the pot and stir so they don't stick together .
- Then add lemon juice, salt to taste, 1 cup of olive oil and stir.
- Pour the tutnajeh into small glass bowls and garnish with fried bread and
coriander.
- This meal is served for lunch and dinner.

2. *Kishik* with *Burghol* (cracked wheat)

This dish is served for breakfast along with green onions and radishes. The inhabitants of Urbeen don't eat the usual Damascene breakfast of bread, yogurt, cheese and olives.

Although it bears the name of "*Kishik* with *Burghol*" it doesn't include the *burghol* in its ingredients. The reason for this is that a long time ago, women used to grab a handful of *burghol* and throw it into the boiling pot. Time passed and they stopped adding *burghol*, but the name stuck.

Ingredients:
  1/2 a cup dried fava beans, skinless soaked over night.
  1 cup lentils.
  4 cups water to boil fava beans and lentils.
  1 teaspoon salt.
  juice of 1 lemon.
  1/2 a cup *kishik*.
  2 large onions, cut into small pieces and fried.
  2 cloves of garlic.
  1 Arabic loaf of fried bread cubes.
  1 tablespoon dried mint.
  1 cup of olive oil.

Method:
- Add the drained fava beans and lentils to 4 cups water. Cook until beans and lentils are tender.
- Add the fried onions, 2 garlic cloves, 1/2 a cup of *kishik* and constantly stir for 10 minutes.

- Add mint, lemon juice, olive oil, fried bread and salt to taste.
- Pour in small glass bowls and serve hot.

The *Muhafaza* of Homs

Homs lies at an altitude of 495 m. above sea level and at a distance of 160 km north of Damascus. It lies midway between Damascus and Aleppo. Homs has been an important city from ancient times although most of its Roman monuments have been destroyed by rebuilding and by violent earthquakes. It retained its importance under the Arab rule and is famous for the tomb of Khalid Ibn Al-Walid, the great commander of the Muslim armies who bought Islam to Syria in 636.

Homs today owes its importance to its economic and strategic position in the middle of the various Syrian regions, in addition to the large number of industrial establishments such as the nearby oil refinery, sugar and cotton factories.

A Folktale from Homs:
The Pomegranate's Secret

Once upon a time, there lived a very rich king who owned vast lands, castles and wealth. One day, this king called his eldest daughter to him and gave her an expensive present and asked her, "Who is the provider?"

The girl thanked her father and said, "You are my only provider."

The king was pleased with his daughter's answer and sent for his second daughter.

The king gave the second daughter a valuable gift and also asked her the same question and she was able to satisfy him as well as the first. But when he called on his youngest daughter Gallia and gave her a present she said in answer to his question, "Allah is the provider of all."

Angered with Gallia's answer he vowed to marry her to the first beggar who came to the door. Soon a poor man carrying a bag knocked at the door begging for food. The king asked his guards to let him in.

When the beggar stood in the presence of the king, he was addressed with the following words: "I will not only give you some food and coins, but I will give you my daughter Gallia for your wife!"

The poor beggar was horror stricken but pleased for who could refuse a princess for a bride.

When the marriage ceremony was completed the king told his daughter Gallia, "You must go with your husband and discover for yourself who is the provider."

Gallia cried and kissed her sisters good bye and followed her poor husband, trusting herself to Allah's protection, sure in the knowledge that Allah would provide her with all she needs.

At last they reached a little mud hut. The poor man said: "This is our house." The beggar's old mother joyfully welcomed them at the door, "Welcome, a thousand welcomes my beloved ones!"

"I have no family but you," said Gallia.

"You are most welcome to our family," said the mother as she embraced Gallia. "I will love you as much as I love my own son, Ahmad."

The next day, Gallia gave her husband Ahmad her only golden coin and asked him to buy them some food.

In a week or so, Gallia spotted a camel caravan passing by their hut. She ran towards it and begged the head of the caravan to take her husband with them. The caravan leader was very impressed by Gallia's politeness and eloquence and agreed to hire her husband and take him along.

One day, the caravan stopped at a well and Ahmad went down to the well to fill up the jugs with water. Suddenly, a scary *Afreet* (a supernatural being) appeared carrying a pomegranate.

"Don't be scared!" said the *Afreet*. "Send this pomegranate to your wife Gallia."

Ahmad thanked the *Afreet* and sent the pomegranate along with some money to Gallia. When Gallia received the pomegranate, she opened it and found inside the most precious diamond she had ever set her eyes upon.

The caravan travelled through many cities, and whenever Ahmad went down a well to fill up the jugs with water, an *Afreet* appeared and gave him a pomegranate to send to his wife. In every pomegranate, Gallia found a precious diamond. Soon, Gallia had enough money to build a castle larger than her father's castle and to fill it with rich furniture.

When her husband Ahmad retuned back from his journey, he couldn't believe his eyes. "What is the secret of this fantastic castle?" he asked.

"The secret is in the pomegranates that you often sent me. Each one enclosed a large, valuable diamond!"

Ahmad knelt down to the ground and thanked Allah for everything He had given them.

As time passed, the news of Gallia and Ahmad was carried from tongue to tongue and the king heard of his daughter's twist of fortune. He decided to come and see with his own eyes whether it was really his own daughter who was living like a queen. When he arrived, he saw a castle which out-did his own. His daughter ran towards him and kissed his hand and invited him into her castle.

The king was greatly affected and asked his daughter to forgive him and said, "You were right, my daughter. Allah is the provider of us all! There is no provider in this world but Allah!"

Riddle

A house with no door
Is inhabited by men
Inside there are four.
What is it? Answer: a walnut

A Recipe from Homs: *Sitt Izmeh-ee*

Sitt means "Lady" and *Izmeh-ee* means "slide down." This tasty dish probably acquired its name because it is easily swallowed and digested.

Ingredients:
- 1 cup of drained and soaked lentils.
- 8 cups of water.
- 1 teaspoon of salt.
- 1 teaspoon of pepper.
- 2 pounds of ground lamb.
- 1 large onion.
- 3/4 of a cup of butter.
- 2 cups of flour.
- 2 cups of lukewarm water
- 1/2 a teaspoon of salt.

Method:
- Dice the onion and fry it in butter until soft. Then add the meat and fry.
- Boil the lentils in the 8 cups of salted water for 45 minutes until soft then drain and set aside.
- Mix the lentils with onion and meat and season with salt and pepper.
- Mix 2 cups of flour with 2 cups of lukewarm water and 1/2 a teaspoon ofsalt.
-Then knead well and roll with a rolling pin.
- Place the mixture on the dough and roll it up like a jelly roll.
- Slice the rolled up dough into small pieces.
- Boil the lentil water and add the slices of dough and cook until they are done.

The *Sitt Izmeh-ee* Song:

This song is sung by the woman who is cooking *Sitt Izmeh-ee,* with a chorus sung by the young girls who are helping her.

Woman:	*Sitti* slide down!
Young girls:	She will not slide down!
Woman:	My eye* slide down!
Young girls:	I will not slide down!
Woman:	My soul* slide down!
Young girls:	I will not slide down!
Woman:	My heart* slide down!
Young girls:	I will not slide down!

---

*In Arabic "my eye", "my soul" and "my heart" are all terms of endearment.

The *Muhafaza* of Hama

Hama is at an altitude of 300 m and a distance of 200 km north of Damascus. It is a very ancient city on the banks of the river Orontes and dates back at least to the fourth millennium B.C when the Amorites lived in this place Later on, the Hitties, Assyrians, Babylonians, Persians, Greeks, Romans and Byzantines all settled there. Finally with the dawn of Islam, the Arabs arrived and Islamic civilization flourished.

Hama is well known for the enormous wooden water wheels on the Orontes river which are centuries old. As these wheels turn and draw water from the river, they make a unique sound which can be heard from afar. The sound of the wheels groaning as they constantly turn is a sound you will never forget. Hama is also known for its traditional industries especially textiles and cotton cloth.

The most important sites in Hama in addition to the water wheels are the Great Mosque, the Azem Palace, the Old Citadel and the Al-Nouri Mosque.

A Folktale from Hama: The Cow Who Lied

Once upon a time, there lived an old man who had three sons and only one cow. Every day, one of the three sons would take the cow to graze in the meadow from morning until sunset.

One day, the old man asked the cow, "Are my sons feeding you well?"

"No!" said the cow. "Your sons are starving me to death. I haven't had anything to eat or drink for days!"

The old man was in rage and threw his three sons out of the house. The three brothers found jobs at different places. The eldest brother, Ahmad, worked in a bakery, the second brother, Sameer, worked in a grocery store, while the third brother, Farouk, worked at a mill.

As years passed, Ahmad felt homesick and missed his father and wished to visit him. When his master heard of his wish he presented him with a horse.

"You've served me so well," said the baker, "that I want to reward you with this pony which has a wonderful gift. All you have to do is feed it a walnut and gold coins will pour out of its mouth"

Ahmad was overjoyed and thanked the baker for his kindness and went off on his journey.

On his way he stopped to eat and spend the night at a khan. When Ahmad was asked to pay for his dinner, he fed his pony a walnut and golden coins poured out of his pony's mouth. The servant's eyes dazzled as he watched the golden coins in Ahmad's hands and secretly decided to steal the pony.

At night, while Ahmad was soundly asleep, the servant crept into the room and stole the pony.

In the morning, Ahmad woke up to find that the pony had disappeared. When he asked the servant if he had seen it, he said that he saw it run towards the forest.

In the mean time, Sameer had also missed his father and expressed his wish to visit him. His master presented him with a table and said, "I'm very pleased with you and your work that is why I want to give you a special present. This table is not an ordinary one, for once you place it before you and say: 'Table, I want some chicken' - a chicken, or what ever else you order, will appear on the table."

Sameer thanked the grocer for his kindness and started travelling towards his father's house. On his way, he felt a little tired and by chance he went into the same khan in which his brother Ahmad had spent the night.

When Sameer ordered the servant to bring him some fish, the servant apologized and said they didn't have any.

So Sameer placed the table in front of him and said: "Table, I want fish!" To the servant's amazement, a big dish of fish appeared on the table.

At night, the servant slipped into Sameer's room and stole the table. In the morning, Sameer woke up and didn't find his precious table. When he confronted the servant, he denied he had taken the table.

Later on, Ahmad and Sameer met at the house of their younger brother, Farouk. They told him about the dishonest servant who had stolen their pony and table.

"Don't worry," said Farouk. "I'll meet you at the khan this evening."

Then Farouk met his master and expressed his wish to go and visit his old father. The miller gave him a sack and said, "I'm very pleased with your work and that's why I want to give you this sack. This sack is very special for it has a stick inside of it. If you are in trouble, all you have to do is say: 'Stick stick… come out stick' and at once the stick will come out of the sack and do as you want. Be careful though, for it will not stop and return to the sack until you tell it so."

Farouk thanked his master and joined his brothers at the khan.

As the three brothers sat at the table, the younger brother asked the servant where he had hid the pony and the table that he had stolen from his brothers.

"I didn't steal your brothers' pony and table!" said the servant.

Farouk called out loudly: "Stick stick come out of the sack!" Suddenly, a stick jumped out of the sack and started to beat the servant.

"Stop, stop that stick!" shouted the servant.

"You must first return the pony and the table to us!" said Farouk.

"Please send the stick back to the sack and I'll return the pony and the table right away!" cried the servant.

Once the servant returned the table and the pony back to them, the three brothers travelled together to visit their father.

The father was so happy to have his three sons back home with him. As he embraced them, he told them that the cow had died a few months ago. As it was dying, the cow had confessed that it had lied to him and that his sons had fed her well."

The three brothers gave their father the pony, table and sack and they all lived together happily ever after.

Riddle

Bowl within a bowl
Floating in the sea
White from within
And brown is its skin.
What is it? Answer: an onion

A Recipe from Hama: *Barasia* (Leeks) with Meat

Ingredients:
1 kilo leeks.
2 carrots.
2 pounds of cubed lamb.
1 bunch of coriander (*kizbara*) or a tablespoon of dried coriander.
10 cloves of garlic.
salt and pepper to taste.
1 lemon.

Method:
- Slice leeks, wash and drain.
- Peel carrots and cut into small slices.
- Cook meat until almost done, and then add leeks and carrots.

- Mash the garlic and coriander in mortar then add when the leeks are done and cook for 3 minutes.
- Serve on a plate with lemon juice and eat with Arabic bread.

Hadith

Miqdad bin Maid Yakreb relates that the Holy Prophet (pbuh) said, " No food tastes better than that which one has earned from the toil of his own hands.

Reported by Bukhari

The *Muhafaza* of Idlib

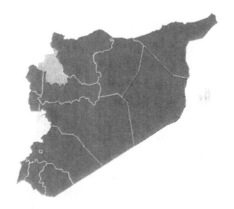

Idlib is located 55 km. west of Aleppo. It is well known for its olive oil, wheat, cotton and its orchards of olive, cherry and fig trees. It is also famous for its mineral water baths.

It has many archeological sites especially the nearby ruins of the ancient city of Ebla which goes back to the second and third millenniums B.C.

A Folktale from Idlib: The Fortune

Once upon a time, there lived a very poor man who would sometimes find a job for one day and then for ten days he would find no work and go hungry. Some days there was nothing in the house to eat.

One morning, as he was desperately looking for work to feed himself and his pregnant wife, a camel caravan heading towards the city of Damascus passed by him. One of the men of the caravan looked at him compassionately and said, "Travel to Damascus... it's easy to find a job there."

The man ran back home and said to his wife: "Prepare yourself we are going to Damascus tomorrow morning!"

"What!" exclaimed his wife "Can't you see the state I'm in? I might give birth any time."

"We're traveling for the sake of our child," said the man "His fortune is in Damascus."

The next day, the man and his wife started out on their journey to Damascus, traveling on a mule. It took them four days to reach the outskirts of Damascus where they met a merchant. The poor man introduced himself to the merchant as a very wealthy man who would soon be followed by a caravan loaded with costly goods.

"I'm looking for a house to buy," said the poor man "but I can't pay for it until my caravan reaches Damascus."

"I have just the right house for you," said the merchant and led him to an old house. Although the house was in bad shape and the walls were about to fall, the man had no choice but to accept since his wife was about to give birth..

That night, the man's wife gave birth to a well formed healthy boy, who was like a full moon on the night of fourteenth.

The man was very happy but concerned at the same time. His new born son needed clothes and food and he was penniless.

"I need to find something to wrap my baby in," said the man to himself as he wandered around the house from room to room.

Suddenly he saw an old piece of cloth tucked into a hole in the wall. The man grabbed the cloth with his hand and pulled as hard as he could. To his amazement, as he pulled, gold coins tumbled out into his hands.

Amazed the man reached his hand into the hole and found a tin can full of gold coins.

"*Al Hamdu Lillah! Al Hamdu Lillah*!" said the man as he danced joyfully.

Now he realized he could buy new clothes for his baby, pay for the house, buy everything the house lacked, and provide a comfortable life for his family.

He ran to his wife and sang joyfully, "Didn't I tell you that our son's fortune would be in Damascus?"

Later on, the man bought a large store in the center of the city, and through his trade and hard work became rich and prosperous and he and his wife and son lived happily ever after.

Riddle

Soaked with fat on the outside
Thin and slim on the inside
Hey hey, feed us this way
Every day, not only today!
What is it? Answer: *kibbeh*

Three Recipes from Idlib:

1) *Kibbeh Sferjalieh* (Quince *Kibbeh*)

Sferjalieh Sauce – Ingredients:
　　4 quinces.
　　1 pound of lamb cut into 1- inch cubes.
　　1 tablespoon of butter.
　　1 tablespoon of tomato paste.
　　3 tablespoons of pomegranate molasses.
　　salt according to taste.

Method:
- Brown meat with a tablespoon of butter until brown.
- Cut and wash the quinces into small cubes without peeling them.
- Add the quince cubes to the meat and sauté them.
- Add water enough to cover the meat and quince slices.
- Poach the quince until soft.
- Add the tomato paste, pomegranate molasses, and salt and cook until the sauce thickens.

Kibbeh Filling – Ingredients:
　　1 pound of ground lamb.
　　1 medium onion finely chopped.
　　4 tablespoons of butter.
　　1/2 a teaspoon of cinnamon.
　　1/2 a teaspoon of pepper.
　　1/2 a cup of pine nuts.

Method:
- Fry onion in oil until golden.
- Add meat and pine nuts, and add a few table-spoons of water to soften the meat.
- Season and add cinnamon.

Kibbeh Shell – Ingredients:
   1 pound of ground lamb.
   1 large onion.
   2 cups of fine *burghol*.
   1/2 a teaspoon of salt.
   1/2 a teaspoon of pepper.
   Oil to fry the *kibbeh*.

Method:
- Rinse the *burghol* in a pan of water then drain the water in a strainer and squeeze out all moisture.
- Add the ground meat, onions, salt and pepper to the *burghol*.
- Grind and knead all ingredients together well by hand until smooth and moist.
- Wet your hand with cold water and take a small lump of *kibbeh* mixture. Hold it in your left hand and make a hole with your finger then widen the hole and flatten the walls until a hollow oval shape is formed.
- Fill the shell with the filling.
- Close by sticking the edges together.
- Add the *kibbeh* to the sauce and cook for 5 minutes until it is done.

This dish can be prepared without the *kibbeh* and served with rice.

2) *Ikseb wa Halawa*

This kind of sweet is very old. In the early twentieth century school children in Idlib used to buy it from street peddlers standing next to their school gates.

Method:
- Sesame seeds are ground and oil, tahina, and the sticky, gluey remains of the seeds are obtained. The remains of these seeds are mixed and kneaded together until they form a doughy substance.
- This doughy substance is formed by hand into cones, similar to ice cream cones. These cones are called *aboot*. -The cones are then filled with *halawa* (halva).

3) *Al Eesh* (*Burghol* with Vine Leaves)

Ingredients:
fresh young vine leaves.
1 and 1/2 a cup of fine *burghol*.
3 cups of water.
juice of 1 lemon.
1 tablespoon of tomato paste.
3 tablespoons of pomegranate molasses.
1 medium onion.
3 tablespoons of olive oil.
Salt and cumin seed to taste.

Method:
- Pick (or buy) grape leaves when they are young and tender.
- Wash the vine leaves thoroughly and cut off stalks.

- Boil 3 cups of water and drop the vine leaves in face up.
- Remove the leaves one by one after boiling for a few minutes.
- Cool slightly and set aside.
- Cool the water in which the vine leaves were boiled in, then soak the *burghol* for 1/2 hour in this water.
- Drain and squeeze the *burghol* well and put it in a large mixing bowl.
- Add the lemon juice, tomato paste, and pomegranate molasses and mix well.
- Mince the onion fine and fry in olive oil and then add the onion to the other ingredients and mix well.
- Season with salt and cumin seed and serve in a salad bowl.
- This dish is not eaten with spoons or bread. Use the vine leaves to scoop up mouthfuls of the *eesh*.

A song chanted by street peddlers selling quince

Oh quince,
On every bite of you
We choke!
Brought from Al Ashrafieh Al Wadi
Oh quince
You refresh one's heart!
Help yourself to a quince -
You who want to make up
With your mother-in-law!*

---

*Eating a raw quince usually makes you choke. Therefore, one wonders whether the street peddler intends for you to make up with your mother in law or to make her choke and die and thus get rid of her!

Halawa Street Peddler Chant

Sweeten your tooth young child!

The *Mohafaza* of Aleppo

Aleppo is situated 350 km north of Damascus and one of the oldest inhabited cities in the world. It was successively occupied by Hittites, Egyptians, Assyrians, Babylonians, Greeks, Romans, Byzantines and finally Arabs.

It became a flourishing city during the Ottoman period because it was a vital connection between the Asian and African provinces of the Ottoman Empire and the capitol city, Istanbul.

Aleppo has many ancient monuments and such as the Aleppo Citadel and its gates including Bab Al-Faraj, Bab Al Naser, Bab Qinnisrin and Bab Al Takieh. There are also beautiful palaces, mosques and churches.

The city is also the center for textile industries including cotton, silk and wool because of its position adjoining the farmlands of the Euphrates Valley and Al-Jazira. Fruit preserves are also a specialty of the city.

A Folktale from Aleppo: The Sly Fox

It was a very cold and rainy night. The wind blew fiercely as the hungry fox ran through the fields. To his disappointment every henhouse in town was locked. There was no way for him to slip through the locked doors and snatch a chicken or a duck.

The poor fox had to run back into his cave empty-handed and spend the night plotting for his breakfast. The next morning, the fox leaped out of his cave and wrapped a white bandage around his head while dragging a stick behind him.

The rooster was the first to see the fox "What are you up to, dear fox?" asked the puzzled rooster.

"Didn't you know?" asked the Fox "I have repented of all my sins and decided to go on Hajj to Mecca."

"You go on Hajj! I can't believe it!" said the Rooster in amazement.

"O yes, indeed." said the fox.

"May I go along with you?" asked the rooster. "I'd love to go and see the Kaaba!"

"Yes, of course," said the fox. "Hop on the stick behind me."

"I'm afraid you'll eat me." said the rooster.

"O no, I can't! I am going to become a hajji and have repented from eating chicken!"

The rooster hesitated then hopped on the stick behind the fox. They both went along until they met the hen.

The hen was scratching for food in the farmyard and was shocked to see the rooster sitting on a stick behind the fox.

"Where are you going?" asked the hen.

"We are going on Hajj to Mecca!" said the fox and the rooster.

"Ya Allah! Can I go with you?" said the hen.

"Certainly!" said the Fox fiendishly. "There is a place for everyone."

The hen hopped on the stick behind the rooster and they went along until they met the duck.

"Quack, quack," said the duck. "Where are you heading to?"

"Oh we're going on Hajj to Mecca," answered the hen. "Do you want to go with us?"

"O yes!" said the duck and hopped on the stick behind the hen.

They walked and walked until they reached the fox's cave. The fox pointed at the cave and said, "This is a short-cut to Mecca!"

The rooster, the hen and the duck hesitated and said, "We're afraid that you are tricking us."

"Me? No I'm a Hajji! How many times do I have to tell you that I have repented?"

The fox entered the cave and they followed him. Once the rooster, the hen and the duck were inside the cave, the fox leaped at the rooster and the hen and snapped off their heads. The poor duck stood in the corner trembling.

"Please," begged the duck. "Let me just go to the river and drink some water before you eat me."

The fox felt very thirsty after he had eaten the rooster and the hen, so he agreed to accompany the duck to the river.

When they reached the river, the duck jumped into the water and the fox leaped after her. The duck swam away and called out, "You must stop lying and tricking your friends before you think of going to Hajj." Then she dove into the water and swam away.

The fox could not swim and began to scream for help, but of course no one came to pull him out and soon he drowned. And that was the end of the sly fox and his crooked tricks.

Riddle

My finger is yellow
I'm not cheap!
Bite me off
Yike, my shirt
Comes off...
What am I? Answer: banana

A Recipe from Aleppo:
Rushtaya (Vermicelli Custard)

Ingredients:
    1/4 of a cup of vermicelli.
    5 cups of milk and 1/2 a cup of water.
    6 tablespoons of sugar.
    3 tablespoons of cornstarch

3/4 of a teaspoon of orange-blossom water.

Method:
- Heat water and add 1/4 cup of vermicelli until it boils, then drain.
- Mix 5 cups of milk with the 1/2 cup of water then heat about 10 minutes, constantly stirring until it boils.
- Add the vermicelli to the milk and cook on a low fire and stir with a wooden spoon so that it does not stick to the pan.
- Mix the cornstarch with a little water to make a paste then add to the milk- vermicelli mixture. Then add sugar and stir until it begins to get thick. Then add orange blossom water and remove from fire and pour into bowls and serve cold.

Hadith

Abu Hurairah relates that the Holy Prophet (pbuh) said: The food of two persons suffices for three and the food of three is enough to feed four.

–Reported by Bukhari and Muslim-

Muna Imady

The *Muhafaza* of Latakia

Latakia is called the bride of the Mediterranean Sea and the gem of the Syrian coast. It was established by Seleucos Nictar, one of Alexander the Great's generals and the first Seleucide king. King Seleucos named the city it after his mother, Laudetia

Located on the north of the Syrian coast, it is the main and busiest Syrian seaport on the Mediterranean. It receives the major part of Syria's imports and from this city Syria exports its agricultural and mineral products to foreign markets.

It is well known for its Citadel of Saladin, Al-Madeeq Citadel and for Ugarit (Ras Shamra) where the oldest alphabet in the world was discovered.

A Folktale from Latakia:
Tunnay and *Runnay*

Once upon a time, a miserably sad man was travelling in the desert when he came upon another unhappy traveler.

"My name is Insi," the first man said. "What's your name?"

"My name is Jinni," answered the other man, who was really a jinn with magical powers.

"Why are you so miserable?" asked Insi.

"I no longer can endure life with my wife, Runnay," said Jinni. "Ever since we got married, she's been quarreling with me day and night."

"That's odd!" Insi interrupted him.

"Why so?" asked Jinni.

"I have left my house for the same reason! My wife Tunnay has driven me crazy... I just can't take it anymore. I'm here in the desert to seek peace from her."

The two men laughed and sat down and started to talk about their unhappy marriages. They soon became good friends and decided to be partners in a scheme to get rich.

"We will choose a wealthy girl." said Jinni, "and, with my powers, I will make her lose her mind. Then you will come along and claim to her family that you can cure her. With a gesture from you I'll cure her, and then we will divide the fee between us."

Things went smoothly as they both planned and they made a lot of money until one day Jinni made the King's daughter lose her mind. The King was very concerned for his daughter and announced that he would marry her to the man who could cure her.

Insi came along and introduced himself to the King and promised to cure his daughter. He then made the gesture for Jinni to do his work. Once the princess was cured, Insi took credit for curing the princess and married her himself.

When Jinni saw that Insi had betrayed him and married the princess, he was furious and decided to get his revenge on Insi. He went to the daughter of the King's wazir and made her lose her mind.

Of course, the wazir went running to Insi who was now famous for his ability to cure insanity. "Please," pleaded the wazir to Insi. "You must cure my daughter like you cured the princess!"

Insi was at a loss for he knew that Jinni would never agree to help him after he had betrayed him.

Suddenly he thought of a great idea and he turned to the wazir and asked him, "Have you got any cannons?"

"Yes, of course!" said the wazir.

"Then," said Insi, "order your men to fire the cannons all at once!"

As soon as the canmons were fired, Jinni rushed to Insi and asked, "What's all this terrible clatter?"

Insi looked at Jinni and said, "Haven't you heard? Runnay and Tunnay have arrived in the kingdom!"

"O no not Runnay again!" screamed Jinni and he ran out of the kingdom as fast as he could. Of course, neither Runnay nor Tunnay had really showed up, but once Jinni left the kingdom, the wazir's daughter immediately regained her sanity and as for Jinni, no one ever saw him again.

To this day, whenever Syrians are told something important has happened and then find out the story was greatly exaggerated, that a big fuss has been made out of nothing, they exclaim: "*Shu hel tunnay wal runnay?*" ("What's this Tunnay and Runnay?")

Riddle

My daughter in the meadow
Shivers: brrr it's cold!
Though she's dressed
In so many robes!
What is it? Answer: a cabbage

Two Recipes from Latakia:

1) Turkey or chicken *Hariseh* (Mashed Turkey or Chicken)

This plate is usually prepared during the celebrations of New Year.

Ingredients:
　　4 cups of wheat soaked overnight.
　　1/2 a turkey or chicken breast cut into cubes.
　　1/4 of a pound of lamb cubes.
　　Salt and butter according to taste.

Method:
- Boil the turkey and meat then add the wheat and cook until it is done.
- Place the turkey breast, meat and wheat in a mortar and pound it well.

- Return the mashed mixture back to the pot and constantly stir until it gets thick.
- Add some butter and salt to taste then cook for 10 minutes.
- Serve it hot.

2) *Lubyia* (Black-Eyed Peas) with *Silq* (Swiss Chard)

Ingredients:

1 cup of black-eyed peas (with the pods)
2 pounds of Swiss chard.
1 cup of olive oil.
1 onion.
15 cloves of garlic.
1 tablespoon of dried coriander
1 lemon.

Method:

- Cook beans then wash the Swiss chard and cut into small slices and add to the black-eyed peas to cook.
- Cut the onion into large slices and fry in olive oil along with 5 garlic cloves and set aside.
- Mash the 10 cloves of garlic with coriander in a mortar and then fry in oil.
- Add the black-eyed peas and Swiss chard to the frying pan and turn over for 5 minutes.

Serve cold on a plate decorated with slices of lemon.

Hadith

Omar bnu Abi Salama said: Recite the name of Allah, the Exalted. Eat with your right hand, and eat from what is in front of you.

-Reported by Bukhari and Muslim.

Hadith

Bara'a bin Azib relates that the Holy Prophet (pbuh) said: When two Muslims meet and shake hands, they are forgiven their sins before they part.

-Reported by Abu Daud.

The *Muhafaza* of Tartus

Tartus is the second important port of Syria on the Mediterranean Sea. It was called "Antaradus" by the Phoenicians and "Tartusa" by the Byzantines.

Since the city dates back more than 6000 years ago, it is full of archeological and historical monuments. It was liberated by the Arabs from the Byzantine rule at the dawn of Islam. Then it was reoccupied by the Byzantine Emperor Nicephor Phokas and liberated again by the Fatimids. Later it was occupied by the Crusaders and remained one of their last strongholds in the East until it was liberated by the Mamluk Sultan Kalawoon in 1291 A.D.

Among the important monuments are the Tartus Citadel and the Great Mosque. The city also possesses the most ancient icon of Virgin Mary made by Saint Luke and the oldest altar consecrated by Saint Peter. These items are in the Chapel of Tartus.

Two Folktales from Tartus:

1) The Old Woman and the Black Cat

Once upon a time, there lived an old woman who possessed nothing in this world but a cow. Every morning, she would gather grass and feed the cow. Then in the evening, she would milk the cow and heat the milk for breakfast.

One day, a black cat crept into the old woman's cottage and drank all the milk. The poor old woman came back and didn't find a drop of milk. The next night and the night after that, the same thing happened.

"I will hide behind the closet and see who is drinking my milk," said the old woman to herself. Then picked up a big broom and hid behind the closet.

Soon the black cat crept inside the cottage and headed for the milk. While the cat was drinking, the old woman swung her broom angrily and hit him so hard that his tail went flying to the other side of the room.

"Meow! Meow!" cried the cat. "Give me back my tail… I can't go back to town without my tail! My town is far away and I must reach it before sunset."

The old woman picked up the cat's tail and swung it joyfully and said, "You must give me back my milk, and then I'll give you back your tail!"

So the cat went to the cow and said: "Will you give me some milk for the old woman so she'll give me back my tail? I must reach my town before sunset"

"I can't give you some milk until you bring me some mulberry leaves," said the cow.

The poor cat went to the mulberry tree and said, "O mulberry tree, please drop me some of your leaves for the cow, so that she'll give me some milk to take to the old lady so that she'll give me back my tail."

The mulberry tree said, "I can't give you some of my leaves until I quench my thirst."

So the black cat ran to the spring and begged it to water the mulberry tree. "O please spring," said the cat, please let your water overflow so the mulberry tree may quench its thirst and drop me some leaves to take to the cow so the cow can give me some milk to give to the old lady so she'll give me back my tail! I must return to my town before sunset."

"Bring me some children to play and jump around me," said the spring. "I can only overflow if I'm happy."

So the poor cat went to the village and called upon the children: "O please children, come along with me and play around the spring so it may overflow!"

The children felt sorry for the black cat when she told them the tale of her lost tail and followed it to the spring. The children jumped and played around the spring until its water gushed out and flowed over the fields.

The mulberry tree quenched its thirst and dropped its leaves for the cat; the cat fed the leaves to the cow, and the cow let him have some milk. The cat took the milk to the old woman and she gave him back his tail. The black cat put his tail in its place and ran off happily to his town and was never seen again.

2) *Boujhayesh*

Once upon a time, a donkey by the name of Bojhayesh agreed with a goose, a duck and a pigeon to plant a piece of land.

The goose said, "How about growing rice?"

"No… no let's plant chick peas!" called out the pigeon.

"No… I'd rather plant wheat." argued the duck.

Then Boujhayesh brayed loudly, "The best thing would be to grow barley!"

At last they decided to take everyone's suggestions. They planted rice, chick peas, wheat and barley and agreed that each of the friends would have a turn to water them.

After a couple of days, the goose went to water the field. She checked on the crops and found that they had grown a little.

Next it was the turn of the pigeon. He went and watered the land and found that their crops had grown a little more.

When it was the duck's turn, it watered the field and then munched on the crops a little to see it they were ripe. Then the duck went back to her friends and said, "The rice, chick peas, wheat and barley will be ready to harvest in a week or so."

After a week had passed, Boujhayesh passed by the land and couldn't resist munching and nibbling a little of this and a little of that until he had eaten up everything, leaving nothing for his poor friends.

The next morning, the four friends went to harvest the crop. To their great disappointment, they found nothing left to reap!

Every one of them swore to the other that he had not eaten the crop.

"I have a great idea," said the goose. "Let's go and stand next to the well and swear that we haven't eaten the crop. If we are lying, may we fall into the well!"

The duck, pigeon and Boujhayesh followed the goose to the well. The goose was the first to swear. She called out loud and clear:

"Honk, honk, honk, I'm the goose.

Honk, honk, honk, I eat rice.

Honk, honk, honk, if I have eaten the rice

Honk, honk, honk, may I fall into the well!"

Then it fluttered its wings and safely flew over the well to the house of the *Moukhtar* (the Village Headman).

Then came the pigeon and said:

"Coo, coo, coo, I'm the pigeon

Coo, coo, coo, I eat chick peas

Coo, coo, coo, if I have eaten the chickpeas

Coo, coo, coo, may I fall into the well!"

Then it fluttered its wings and safely flew over the well to the *Moukhtar's* house.

Then came the duck's turn. She stood next to the well and said:

"Quack, quack, quack, I'm the duck

Quack, quack, quack, I eat wheat

Quack, quack, quack, if I have eaten the wheat

Quack, quack, quack, may I fall into the well!"

It fluttered its wings and flew over the well, but its shoes fell into the well.

Finally, Boujhayesh stood at the well unwillingly and brayed:

"Hee haw, hee haw, I'm Bojhayesh

Hee haw, hee haw, I eat barley

Hee haw, hee haw, if I have eaten the barley

Hee haw, hee haw, may I fall into the well!"

Then Boujhayesh tried to jump over the well, but fell into it.

"Please," called out the duck, "throw me back my shoes!"

Boujhayesh threw the duck its pair of shoes and the duck flew to the *Moukhtar's* house.

Then along came a hyena sniffing and sniffing away: "I smell something very good," said the hyena as he neared the well.

Boujhayesh called out from the well, "Pull me out of the well and eat me!"

And the hyena did. When Boujhayesh was out of the well he said to the hyena, "Wash me and eat me!"

But when the hyena picked up the pail and bent towards the well to get some water, Boujhayesh kicked the hyena down into the well.

"Please get me out of here!" called the hyena. "I promise not to eat you!"

Boujhayesh laughed and ran to the *Moukhtar's* house.

"How did you get out of the well?" asked his friends the goose, the duck and the pigeon.

"The hyena pulled me out to eat me, but then I kicked him into the well." said Boujhayesh.

Then Boujhayesh pleaded forgiveness from his friends and said, "I'm really very sorry for what I've done. I feel so ashamed of myself... please forgive me I promise I'll never do it again."

And they did forgive him. Since that day, Boujhayesh, the duck, the goose and the pigeon have remained inseparable and faithful friends.

Riddle

You, who were watered by silver,
And dressed in red,
Why did your family
Sell you so cheap?
What is it? Answer: radishes

Two Recipes from Tartus:

1) *Kibbeh* with Swiss Chard

Ingredients:
2 pounds of Swiss chard.
Olive oil.
1 medium onion and 15 cloves of garlic.
1/2 a teaspoon each of black pepper, salt and cumin.
1/2 a cup of walnuts.
1 cup of fine *burghol*.
1 cup of flour.
1 can of cooked red pepper.
2 lemons.

Kibbeh Filling - Method:
- Wash the Swiss chard, remove the stems and then cut into small pieces.
- Cook the Swiss chard about 6-10 minutes, then squeeze, drain and put aside.

- Heat 3 tablespoons of oil in a pan and fry a medium onion sliced into small pieces. Then add the Swiss chard.
- Cut the walnuts into small pieces then add them to the pan.
- Season with the pepper, salt and cumin and cook for a couple of minutes then set aside to cool.

Kibbeh Shell – Method:
- Wash and soak 1 cup of fine *burghol* in water for 15 minutes then drain in a strainer and squeeze out all moisture.
- Add 1 cup of flour and a sprinkle of salt to the *burghol* and knead together well by hand until smooth and moist.
- Wet your hand with cold water and take a small lump of *kibbeh* mixture. Hold it in your left hand and make a hole with your finger then widen the hole and flatten the walls until a hollow oval shape is formed.
- Fill the shell with the filling.
- Close by sticking the edges together.
- Boil water with 1 teaspoon of salt and drop the *kibbeh* in the water one at a time for about 6 minutes.
- Remove the *kibbeh* from the water and set them aside to cool.

Kibbeh Sauce – Method:
- Mash fifteen cloves of garlic and mix well with the cooked canned red pepper, the juice of 2 lemons and 1/2 a cup of olive oil.
- Pour the sauce over the *kibbeh.*
  This dish is served cold.

2) *Burghol* and Chick Peas

Ingredients:

1 cup of chick peas washed and soaked in water for about 1 and 1/2 hour

2 pounds of boneless chopped beef or lamb.

1 and 1/2 cup rough *burghol,* cleaned and washed.

3 cups of water.

1/2 a cup of olive oil.

2 to 3 tablespoons of butter.

Salt and pepper to taste.

Method:
- Put the meat and the chick peas in a pressure cooker and add three cups of water and cook 45 minutes.
- In another pan melt the butter then add the *burghol* and stir until it turns medium brown.
- Drain the juice of the meat off into three measuring cups, and then add it along with the chick peas to the *burghol.*
- Add salt and pepper then stir, cover and cook on medium fire 15 to 20 minutes until water is absorbed.

- Add half a cup of olive oil and stir for five minutes. Then leave to sit about ten minutes before serving.
- Serve with yogurt and cucumber salad.

Hadith

Aisha relates that the Holy Prophet (pbuh) said, "When any of you begin eating, you should recite the name of Allah, the Exalted. If you forget to do so in the beginning you should say: 'In the name of Allah, first and last'"

-Reported by Tirmizi and Abu Daud.

The *Muhafaza* of Dara'a

It lies 850 km above sea level and 100 km south of Damascus. It is located on the Damascus-Amman highway and is used as a stopping station for travelers.

This province has many archeological sites belonging mostly to the Roman period. The monuments are still well preserved and include the Bosra Amphitheater and the Bosra Citadel.

A Folktale from Dera'a:
The Sky is Raining Meat

Once upon a time, a farmer and his wife lived on a farm. The farmer grew vegetables and fruit and led quite a comfortable life. The only problem he had was that his wife talked too much.

Every day his wife visited all her neighbors and spread all the secrets of their household. The poor farmer felt he couldn't tell her anything without having all the neighborhood hearing about it.

One day, while the farmer was digging in the ground, he found a jug full of ancient gold coins.

"We are rich!" he cried.

But as he grabbed a handful of gold coins he remembered his talkative wife.

"Everyone will hear about this gold sooner or later," he said to himself, "and the *Iktai* (the Landlord) will confiscate it."

So the farmer decided to put the gold back in the ground until he found a way to deal with his talkative wife.

At last, the farmer thought of a good plan and decided to carry it out at once. He secretly killed a sheep and cooked it in the barn. Then climbed up on the roof of their mud house and began dropping big chunks of meat down.

When his wife saw the pieces of meat dropping from the sky, she ran outside and happily gathered up the meat and ate it as she sang;

"The sky is raining meat! The sky is raining meat!"

The same day, the farmer took his wife to the field and dug out the gold coins. "Now", he said, "we will be rich and happy!"

The next day, the wife ran to the neighbors and told them about the gold her husband found in his land.

"My husband has found a treasure!" she happily said to everyone.

The news spread all over the village until it reached the *Iqtai*.

The *Iqtai* went to the farmer and demanded to be given the gold.

"What!" exclaimed the farmer "I don't know what you're talking about!"

His wife looked at him and said, "How could you forget my dear husband? You found the gold the same day it rained meat."

Then the farmer's wife turned to the *Iqtai* and said: "I'm sure you heard about the chunks of meat falling from the sky. Oh, it was so delicious!"

At this the *Iqtai* and the neighbors smiled and shook their heads.

"Meat falling down from the sky!" they exclaimed "You must be crazy."

The *Iqtai* laughed and said, "Now I'm sure there is no gold," and he left.

From that day on, no one ever believed anything the farmer's wife said, and the farmer kept the gold and lived happily ever after.

A Recipe from Dera'a: *Mansaf Burghol*

Ingredients:

4 pounds of cubed boneless lamb meat.

6 cups of rough *burghol*.

5 cups of yogurt.

Salt and pepper to taste.

15 cardamom pods.

2 sticks of cinnamon.

1 onion.

1 tablespoon of corn starch

1/2 a cup of butter.

Method:
- Cook the meat on a low fire and add the onion, the cardamom seeds and cinnamon sticks and cook until the meat is done. Then add salt and pepper to taste.
- Strain the broth to remove the cinnamon sticks, cardamom seeds and the onion
- In a pressure cooker melt the butter then add the *burghol* and stir until it turns medium brown.
- Measure the strained broth and add enough water to make 12 cups of liquid and then pour it on the *burghol* and cover the pressure cooker. When the pressure cooker begins to whistle, reduce the fire to low and allow it to cook for 35 minutes.

Yogurt Sauce – Method:
- Strain yogurt, egg and corn flour into a pan.
- Cook over high heat stirring constantly, until it boils.
- Reduce the heat, simmer for five minutes, stirring occasionally.
- Add the meat and some of the juice of the meat.
- Put the *burghol* in a big serving plate then pour the yogurt on it.
- This dish is usually served with fried *kibbeh*, green onion and green pepper.
  It will serve a large number of people.

Hadith

Ubaidullah Ibn Mohsin Al Ansari Al Khitmi relates that the Holy Prophet (pbuh) said: He who goes to bed enjoying health, safety, and enough to eat for that day is like one who owns the whole world and all it contains.

Reported by Tirmizi

Riddle

Something sparkled
Then hid behind the leaves
O fruit seller, have you seen
Fruit with no leaves?
What is it? Answer: truffles

Muna Imady

The *Muhafaza* of Sweida

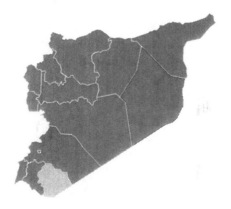

Sweida is a beautiful province and is situated 90 km southeast of Damascus at an altitude of 1100 m. It is in an area of black basalt stone and many of the homes in Sweida are built from this local stone. It has a long history of Seleucide, Nabatean, Roman and Byzantine occupation. The Nabateans called it *Sawada* (the black) due to its black stone.

It is famous for its ruins, baths, temples and palaces as well as its orchards and vineyards which produce excellent apples, grapes and other fruits.

A Folktale from Sweida: The Homesick Bride

Once upon a time, there lived a king who wanted to get married. He looked east and west for a bride with no luck. He could find no one who caught his eye or captured his heart.

One day, the king went out hunting in the forest with his royal huntsmen. As he wandered away from his companions, he saw the most beautiful girl he had ever set eyes upon. Although the girl was dressed in rags, she enchanted him.

"This is the woman of my dreams!" he thought as he followed her to her cottage. Without any ado, the king asked her father for the girl's hand, and he accepted right away, for who could refuse a king as a husband for their daughter? Her family was overjoyed at her good fortune.

The king took the girl back to his royal palace, where they were married. As time passed, the king made sure she had the best of everything in his palace, however, somehow she couldn't forget the happy days she had spent with her family and became more and more homesick.

Every day, when she sat at the table to eat she would close her eyes and say: "Nothing is as good as my family's *muzanara*!"

At night, when she lay on her soft royal bed she would sigh and say to the king, "Oh how I miss sleeping in my family's home on the *jallekh*!"

Finally, the king got tired of hearing these complaints and he decided to take his wife back home and see for himself the wonderful things she was missing. When they arrived at her parents' little hut, the bride took the king to the *tannour* (outdoor mud brick oven) behind the cottage where her mother was baking fresh bread. The bride took a loaf of the round flat bread and picked a fresh green onion from their field and rolled the bread around it into a sandwich. Then she took a big bite and said to the king, "Now this is my family's *muzanara* that tastes better than any royal food I ever ate in your palace!"

"I see," said the king. "Now show me what you mean by sleeping on the *jallekh*."

To the king's surprise, his wife led him to a bare room that had nothing in it but a big rectangular flat stone.

"Touch this stone," said his wife. "Do you feel how soft it is? We sharpen our knives on this stone before we kill the sheep. Then at night we all sleep on it. This is what I meant by sleeping on the *jallekh*."

Horrified, the king said, "So! It seems our royal food and soft beds don't suit you! Well, my dear, you can stay here with your family and enjoy your *muzanara* and your *jallekh*, while I go and find a more suitable wife!"

Riddle

O daughter of the king
Chattering behind the door
-No one understands
Whether she speaks
Turkish or Persian!
What is it? Answer: Water pipe or Narghile

A Recipe from Sweida: *Mlehieh*

This dish is very similar to the *'Mansaf Burghol'* dish of Dara'a with some different details.

Ingredients:
   4 pounds boned lamb meet.
   6 cups of rough *burghol*.
   1 onion.
   5 cups of yogurt.
   1 teaspoon of salt and pepper.
   15 cardamom pods.
   2 sticks of cinnamon.
   1 tablespoon of corn flour (corn starch)
   1/2 a cup of butter.
   3 tablespoons of Arabic butter (*semnay*) or ordinary butter.
   1/2 a cup of almonds.
   1 egg.
   1 tablespoon of tumeric

Method:
- Cook the meat on a low fire and add the onion, the cardamom pods, and cinamon sticks. Then add salt and pepper to taste.
- Drain the broth of the meat, discarding the cinnamon sticks, cardamom seeds and the onion.
- In a pressure cooker melt the butter then add the *burghol* and stir until it turns medium brown. Measure the broth and add enough water to make 12 cups of liquid and then add it to the

burghol and close the pressure cooker. When the pressure cooker begins to whistle, reduce the fire to low and allow it to cook for 35 minutes.

Yogurt Sauce - Method
- Put yogurt, egg and corn flour through a strainer into a pan.
- Add the tumeric to the yogurt.
- Cook over high heat stirring constantly until it boils, then add some of the meat to give it flavor. Reduce the heat, simmer for five minutes, stirring occasionally.
- Put the *burghol* in a big serving plate and thoroughly knead with a plate or a big spoon until it becomes like dough then add some cooked yogurt and knead it again.
- Fry the almonds in the three tablespoons of butter and pour them on the *burghol*. Then decorate the dish with the pieces of meat, fried *kibbeh* and green pepper.
- Pour a little of the cooked yogurt on the *burghol*, then pour the rest in small bowls so everyone can serve himself according to his taste.

Hadith

Abu Hurairah relates that the Holy Prophet (pbuh) said: Among the Muslims the most perfect, as regards his faith, is one whose character is excellent, and the best of you are those who are best to their wives.

Reported by Tirmizi.

Muna Imady

The *Muhafaza* of Al-Quneitra

The word of 'Quneitra' comes from the word "qantara" meaning bridge since Quneitra is a "bridge" connecting Syria, Lebanon and Palestine.

It is 70 km south of Damascus and is known for its abundance of water. It has been settled by man since the Stone Age and thus is rich in archeological monuments from the Hellenistic, Roman, Byzantine and Arab periods.

It was occupied in 1967 by the Israelis and liberated in 1973 during the October war.

Two Folktales from Quneitra:

1) Sherehan Abu Khabeza

Once upon a time there was a man named Sharehan who had ten daughters and no job to support them. Sharehan was a very lazy man who rejected all the proposals for employment he was offered and preferred to wander in the fields and collect wild herbs such as khabeza. Therefore he was known by the name of Sharehan Abu Khabeza.

One spring day, while he was collecting khabeza, an attractive, middle-aged woman ran towards him and cried out: "*Alhamdu lillah* I have found you, my dear brother Hamdan!"

"I'm sorry, but I have no sister." said Sharehan.

The woman looked at him and gasped, "O brother Hamdan, don't you even recognize your poor sister?"

Sharehan shook his head and said: "Sorry but my name is Sharehan... not Hamdan!"

"O they changed your name after they kidnapped you so you would never return back to us! I pity you my poor brother, spending your days collecting khabeza! Believe me you should give yourself a rest and come spend sometime with me and your family and enjoy my wealth!"

Although Sharehan was sure that the woman wasn't his sister, he fancied the idea of enjoying life without work. So Sharehan went back home and told his wife that she should get the family ready for a visit to his wealthy sister.

His wise wife shook her head and said, "Everyone in the village knows that your entire family perished from some kind of mysterious illness and that you were raised by my uncle."

"No!" insisted Sharehan. "She must be my sister. Only a sister would be so warm and loving."

His wife tried to reason with him in vain and at last she was forced to gather her daughters and follow him.

The Ameh (paternal aunt) received Sharehan and his family warmly and showered them with kisses and sweet words, then led them into her house to a great feast that awaited them.

As the days gently passed, Sharehan spent his time sitting in the shade drinking tea. Nevertheless, his wife grew more suspicious day after day, for sometimes she would hear howls from her sister-in-law's room that made the walls of their bedroom tremble.

One day, the oldest daughter was sent to her Ameh with some food. To her great shock, she saw, instead of her Ameh, a *gouleh* devouring a dead human body. The Ameh flashed her red eyes and waved her hairy arms towards the girl and then scratched her with her long sharp nails and growled, "Don't you dare to breathe a word of what you have seen to anyone!"

The girl went running to her bed shivering with fear and cried herself to sleep. In the morning she whispered to her mother what had happened to her. When her mother repeated the story to her husband he shook his head disbelievingly and said, "What a childish story! It seems that your fears have affected our daughters. I will never leave my loving sister ever!"

The next day, the wife took her daughters and some laundry and said they were going to the wadi to wash their clothes in the stream. As soon as they were out of sight they ran as fast as they could to their village and never returned again.

The *ghouleh* waited impatiently for their return, but by the end of the day, she lost hope of them ever coming back.

She howled so loud that Sharehan jumped out of his chair and sought frantically for a shelter.

Suddenly, the *ghouleh* appeared in front of him and slipped off her gown. Sharehan couldn't believe what he saw and before he could blink an eye, she grabbed him and sunk her teeth in his flesh.

The *ghouleh* said joyfully, "Tell me, Sharehan, where shall I start to eat you?"

"Start with my beard because I didn't listen to my wise wife!" said Sharehan.

"And then?" said the *ghouleh*.

"Then eat my two legs because I didn't listen to my poor daughter!"

"And then?" said the *ghouleh*.

"Then eat my hands for being so lazy!"

So the *ghouleh* gobbled lazy Sharehan all up until nothing at all was left of him.

2) The Enchanted Snake

There was once upon a time a shepherd who had a beautiful daughter and two sons. Every morning, his daughter Sheeha drove the sheep in front of her and went out into the fields where the long grass grew. There, she would stay until sunset.

One morning, when Sheeha went out into the fields, she sat down under a tree and watched the sheep graze around her. She was so tired by the long walk in the hot weather that she fell asleep. When she woke up, the sun was setting behind the mountain and the sheep had run far and wide. Not a one was in sight.

"Oh my God!" Sheeha said. "I can't go back home without the sheep. I have to find them!"

While Sheeha walked towards the mountain, she heard a bleet. "They must be somewhere near here," Sheeha said to herself. But when she finally reached the mountain, it was dark and there were no sheep in sight.

Sheeha looked around and saw a cave at the foot of the mountain with a dim light shining from inside.

"The sheep must have entered the cave," Sheeha thought as she took a deep breath and walked into the cave.

As she stepped into the cave it became wider and brighter. Small spiders swung on cobwebs that hung from the ceiling of the cave and mice went in and out of crevasses in the walls of the cave.

Suddenly she heard an unholy scream that made her hair stand up in fear. She looked in the direction of the scream and, to her shock, she saw an old *gouleh* sprinkling powder into a big boiling pot. The *gouleh* was wearing a black silk dress and had red hair that fell wildly to her waist. Her eyes glowed and flashed like fire.

"I've been waiting for you for years!" cackled the *gouleh* as she let out another wild scream and waved her arms in the air.

"I want you to be my helper! Together we'll turn people's lives into hell!"

"No!" Sheeha said, "I'll never do anything like that!"

Hearing Sheeha's words, the *gouleh* fell into a black and terrible rage. She gnashed her teeth and said with a threatening laugh: "Then I will turn you into a snake!"

"There is no magic that can stop me from leaving this cave!" said Sheeha.

"A snake you shall be!" The *gouleh* shrieked as she mumbled magic words and made circles with her hands. All of a sudden, Sheeha turned into a big, scary snake.

"You will remain in this form until you find someone that is courageous enough to jump over your back three times. Remember, the more people are scared of you, the uglier you will become! "

Sheeha was horrified with her new transformation. She slithered along towards her house, but her parents and brothers were frightened of the big, ugly snake and ran away from it.

In despair, Sheeha returned to the cave to beg the *gouleh* to break the spell, but the *gouleh* had disappeared.

So Sheeha began a new life, living alone in the cave. With time she discovered twelve passages in the cave that each led to a secret room full of gold and diamonds.

"What good are gold and diamonds for a wretched old snake like me," said Sheeha to herself bitterly.

Time passed. Sheeha spent her days sunning herself on a rock, or weaving her sinuous, slim body along the fields. One day while she was lying on a rock in the sun, she saw three young men approaching her.

They were startled when they heard the snake talking to them, "Please, don't be frightened by my appearance... I will give you a lot of gold and diamonds if you only jump over me three times!"

Reluctantly, the three young men agreed to give it a try. The first two young men jumped over Sheeha only once. They were both so clumsy with fear that they fell down and didn't want to try again. Then it was the turn of the handsome young man who had no fear of the large snake. He jumped over the snake three times in a row as lightly as a deer and landed each time safely on his feet.

At once, to the surprise of the three young men, the snake was covered in a cloud of smoke. It threw off its snake's skin and changed back into a beautiful young women.

The younger two men looked at Sheeha's face and gasped: "You look so much like our lost sister Sheeha... you even have the same freckle on your nose!"

Sheeha ran towards her two brothers and embraced them passionately and told them her story. Then they all went to the cave and carried the diamonds and the gold back to their village. Her parents were overjoyed to see their daughter again after mourning her for years.

Later on, the young handsome man who broke the *gouleh's* spell, asked for Sheeha's hand. Of course her father agreed and after their marriage they lived happily ever after.

Riddle

At the market
I'm seen green
While I turn red
On your head
What am I? Answer: henna

Two Recipes from Quneitra:

1) *Zalabya*

Ingredients:
   4 cups of flour.
   3 cups of milk.
   1 teaspoon of salt
   1 tablespoon of cake yeast.
   1 tablespoon of oil.
   2 tablespoons of anise.
   1 tablespoon of sugar.
   1 teaspoon of *mahlab*.
   Frying oil.
   Granulated sugar.

Method:
- Mix flour, salt, yeast and oil with milk in a bowl.
- knead until the mixture becomes soft.
- Add the *mahlab*, anise and sugar and knead again until it becomes sticky.
- Leave the dough for an hour until it rises.
- Cut into strips 2 inches wide and about 7 inches long.
- Fry the strips in hot oil until golden brown.

- Set the strips in a plate and sprinkle with granulated sugar.

2) *Lizagy*

Ingredients:
   8 cups of flour.
   1/2 a cup of oil.
   1 teaspoon of yeast.
   1 teaspoon of salt.
   3 cups of lukewarm water.

Method:
- Mix flour, oil, yeast, salt and water and let stand
  covered for an hour.
- Cut into 3-inch balls, then leave for another half
  an hour.
- Then with your hand flatten to thinness of pie
  dough.
- Arrange on an oiled baking tray and bake in mod-
  erate oven (350) for 15 minutes or until bottoms
  are golden. Then flip to other side. (Originally,
  lizagy was baked in a *tannour*, an outdoor mud
  brick oven)

Syrup – Ingredients:
   1/2 a cup of Arabic butter (ghee).
   1/2 a cup sugar.

Syrup – Method:
- Heat the Arabic butter then add the sugar and
  stir constantly.

- Pour generously on each *lizagy* pan cake.
- *Lizagy* is served during the feasts.

Street Peddlers' Chant for *Zalabiya*

O sweet Door of Peace, so sweet (one of the
doors to the Prophet's mosque in Madina)
We have *Zalabiya*
And the Prophet has light, so sweet,
Get your supply of *Zalabiya*
Before you leave Sham
O do please carry to him [the Prophet] my best
regards!

Hadith

Jarir bin Abdullah relates that he heard the Holy
Prophet (pbuh) say: One who is devoid of kindness is
devoid of any kind of goodness.

Reported by Muslim

The *Muhafaza* of Deir-al-Zor

Deir-al-Zor stands on the shores of the mighty Euphrates river, 320 km southeast of Aleppo. It is called the pearl of the Euphrates.

It is noted for its oil fields, the groves of trees and shrubs which line the banks of the Euphrates and for its importance as the central town for the surrounding agriculture community.

It includes archeological sites, forts, palaces, towers, temples, churches and mosques. The most important archeological sites around Deir-al-Zor are: Mari, Tell Ashara, Halabieh-zalabieh, Halabieh fortress and Doura Europos.

A Folktale From Deir-al-Zor: The Woodcutter and the Lion

Day after day, the sun shone triumphantly in the sky, cancelling any hope for rain. With no rain, the trees, crops and plants of the land withered and died. People were desperate and grew poorer and poorer.

Even Deir-al-Zor, where the Euphrates river runs through its land forming fertile islands called *huweja* was hit by the heavy drought.

In a small mud brick house at the foot of a hill, lived a woodcutter and his nine children. Every day, the woodcutter went out looking for trees to cut with no luck.

At sunset his hungry children would hopefully wait for his return. Unfortunately, he had nothing to offer them.

"You must find a way to earn your living" said his wife.

"But this has been my job all my life. I'm not cut out to do anything else!" argued the woodcutter.

Now it happened that there was another *huweja* farther off which was crowded with trees and had plenty of grass and plants, but no one dared to approach it. A great lion lived in it and forbid anyone to come near it.

When things really got bad, the woodcutter decided to go to the lion's island.

"I have no solution but to try and go to the lion's *huweja*" he said to his wife.

"It's so dangerous... please don't go!" begged his wife.

"I will die whether I stay here or go to the lion's *huweja*. Let me try my luck!!"

The next morning, the woodcutter rowed his old boat towards the lion's island. When he reached the *huweja*, he was so taken by the fantastic trees that covered the area that he forgot all about the lion.

Suddenly, a great lion leaped in front of him snarling and growling.

"How dare you come into my island! Don't you know what happens to whomever comes into my island!" roared the lion.

The woodcutter fell down to his knees and started to cry: "Please, your majesty the lion, I'm so poor that my nine children haven't had anything to eat for days. I beg for your mercy to pity me and let me cut just a little wood to sell at the market and buy my starving children something to eat! I'm sure you have such a big heart!"

The lion felt sorry for the poor woodcutter "Okay!" roared the lion "You may come here once a week and cut down all the trees you want!"

"O thank you!" said the woodcutter as his tears rolled down his face. Then he got up to his feet and picked up his ax and cut some wood and carried it to his old boat and rowed it back to town to sell it.

His wife and children couldn't believe their eyes when they saw him return back with plenty of food.

That night, the woodcutter, his wife and nine children ate and drank like they never had in their lives.

Ever since that day, the woodcutter went once a week and chopped as much wood as he could carry in his old boat and went to town to sell it.

The price of wood went up since no one but the woodcutter could go into the lion's island.

Little by little, the woodcutter became richer, and his children turned plump and their faces became rosy and round.

Then the day came when the woodcutter became a very wealthy man whose riches were countless. His home was no longer a small mud brick house, but a palace much like the palaces that kings and queens live in. He no longer went to chop wood, but sent his men to carry the wood in large boats.

One day, the woodcutter set up a big party and invited all his friends except for the lion.

From a distance, the lion heard the sound of music and laughter. He smelt the smell of meat being roasted.

"My friend the woodcutter is having a great invitation today. I must honor him and allow him to be to be my host!" roared the lion with great pride.

When the lion arrived at the woodcutter's palace, everyone froze in their place in fear of him. The lion quietly stepped in and sat next to his friend, the woodcutter and said: "A hundred thousand hellos to my dear friend. I have come to honor you by my presence. May Allah grant you wealth and health"

As the lion uttered these words, he opened up his wide mouth and snapped his sharp yellow teeth. A bad smell came out of his mouth and filled the air. This was the closest the woodcutter had ever been to the lion.

"O you really stink!" said the woodcutter "If I were you I wouldn't sit too close to my friends in fear that I might lose them!"

The lion couldn't believe his ears. How could his friend utter these harsh words after all he had done for him!

Without a word, the lion left the party and went off towards his *huweja*.

The next day, when the woodcutter's men arrived at the lion's *huweja*, the lion roared at them fiercely and warned them not to come back again.

The woodcutter was surprised to hear what the lion did to his men and went to talk to the lion.

"What has come to your mind to throw my men out of your *huweja*?" asked the woodcutter.

"I have made a big mistake to consider you my friend. I treated you with kindness but you returned my kindness with your ungratefulness!" said the lion.

The woodcutter tried to explain himself, but the lion interrupted him and called out: "Raise your ax and kill me! I don't deserve to live after I lost my dignity!"

The ungrateful woodcutter raised his ax and thought to himself: "The best thing I could do is to strike him on his head and get rid of him for once and for all!"

As he viciously approached the lion, the lion moved and the ax struck him on his stomach. The lion roared with pain and then ran away behind the bushes.

No one saw the lion after that day, and everyone believed he was dead. The woodcutter considered himself the owner of the *huweja*. He cut down as many trees as he wanted at any time.

One day, as the woodcutter was walking around the *huweja*, he heard a faint growl. To his surprise, the lion suddenly leaped to its hind legs and started to roar: "This is my *huweja*! How dare you come here and chop my trees without my permission!"

"But.. but!" the woodcutter unsuccessfully tried to put his thoughts into words.

"This is the last talk we have together!" said the lion "I don't want to see you here again... or I'll eat you!"

"Wh what do you mean?" stammered the woodcutter "Aren't we friends?"

"No!" roared the lion "Wounds heal in time, but hurtful words cause scars that never heal!"

Riddle

I'm wrinkled
I'm fragile
On my head, I have a straw.
What am I? Answer: a raisen

Two Recipes from Deir-al-Zor

1) Fora - (A Soup)

Fora is made from the leftovers of the wheat harvest which are called *fashek* (ground wheat).

Fashek is added to a great quantity of yogurt and salt and mixed together. Then it is left for a while until it becomes a solid doughy substance.

Then round circles with holes in the middle (like doughnuts) are formed from the dough and are left to dry.

Later on, the round shaped circles are tied by a string and put in a cloth bag.

In the winter, five of these round circles are soaked in water overnight.

In the morning, the dissolved liquid is heated and cooked beans are added to it along with fried garlic.

This soup is served for breakfast in winter because it gives you energy to face the cold weather.

2) *Bamieh* (Okra)

Ingredients:
- 1 pound of boned lamb meat.
- 2 pounds of okra.
- 8 cups of fresh tomato juice.
- 8 - 10 garlic cloves.
- 3/4 cup of lemon juice.
- 3 - 4 tablespoons of oil.
- 1/4 teaspoon of black pepper.
- 1/4 teaspoon of allspice.

Method:
- Wash okra and cut off stems.
- Cook meat with bones until done.
- Brown meat lightly in oil and add salt, pepper and spices.
- Add the okra and fry about two minutes then pour the fresh tomato juice, crushed garlic and cook without adding water for about half an hour.
- When it is done add the lemon juice.
- Place Arabic bread on a big serving plate then pour the okra on top. It is not served with rice.

Hadith

Abu Hurarah has related that the Holy Prophet (pbuh) said: Allah does not look at your body or your appearance, but at your heart and your deeds.

-Reported by Muslim

Muna Imady

The *Muhafaza* of Raqqa

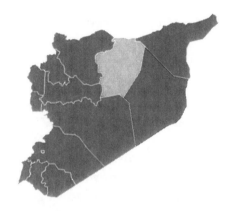

Raqqa stands on the shores of the mighty Euphrates river, along whose banks the most ancient civilization first arose. The city of Raqqa was originally built by Alexander the Great and named Nikephorian in the 4th century B.C but nothing remains of this ancient city. Much later, in 662 A.D., the Abbassid Caliph, Al-Mansur, built a new town on the site of the ruins of old Raqqa. He called his city, Al Rafika and it was adorned by many monuments of Arabo-Islamic architecture during the time of the most famous Abbassid Caliph, Haroun Al-Rashid, who used it as a summer resort.

The most important remains in the city of Raqqa are parts of the surrounding wall and the huge Baghdad Gate, the Palace of the Daughters and the Rafika Mosque.

Al Raqqa is famous for its well-made glass and ceramic ware. It is also has assumed a more important economic role after the completion of the Euphrates Dam in 1974.

Two Folktales From Raqqa:

1) The Raven and the Fox

Once upon a time, a raven invited a fox to be his guest. The fox happily accepted the raven's invitation and came at the appointed time. When the fox arrived, the raven flew up to a date palm tree and plucked and dropped dates down into a thorn bush, saying, "Eat, dear brother, may Allah grant you health!"

Then the raven flew down and again invited the fox to eat. The fox tried to pull out the dates from the thornbush without success for the thorns were as sharp as needles. However, the raven took out date after date with his strong claws.

"Is this what you consider hospitality," said the fox to himself. Nevertheless, he concealed his anger and thanked the raven:

"O my hostess, may Allah reward you for this great feast! said the fox. "I would be honored if you would accept my invitation tomorrow." The raven willingly accepted to come.

The next day, the fox made a delicious porridge and poured it onto a flat rock. Then he slyly said, "Please serve yourself my dear brother, and remember that you should eat a quantity equal to your friendship to me!"

The raven tried to peck at the porridge, but was not able to get one mouthful while the fox licked up every speck of it from the rock.

The raven realized that the fox was returning to him the same kind of invitation he had offered the fox yesterday. Since that day, the raven and the fox have respected one another and considered each other equal in honor and pride.

2) The Just Division

One day, the lion, the fox and the wolf went out hunting in the desert. By the end of the day, they had caught a deer, hare and a pigeon.

As they sat down to rest, the lion roared: "Let's divide the prey among us!"

"By Allah, that's a great idea!" said the wolf and he picked up the pigeon and put it next to the fox and gave the hare to the Lion while he himself, claimed the deer. The wolf stood on the deer and said to the other animals, "What is your opinion of this?"

The lion angrily growled: "You are ignorant in division!" Then he struck the wolf in the face with his great paw.

The wolf wiped at the blood that poured from his face and said, "Well maybe the fox will be more just in dividing the prey!"

The fox looked carefully at the blood pouring from the wolf's face and paused a little before pulling the hare towards the lion as he said, "This will be for my master's breakfast."

Then he pointed at the dead deer and said, "And this will be for my master's supper!"

Then the fox picked up the pigeon and placed it in front of the lion and said, "I also give you this pigeon, dear master, in case you get hungry in between meals!"

The lion was greatly satisfied and said, "You have done well! Who taught you to be so just?"

The fox pointed at the wolf and said, "O great lion, the sight of blood running down the wolf's face taught me a great lesson!"

Hadith

Abu Masud Uqbah ibn Amer Ansari al Badri relates: that the Holy Prophet (pbuh) said: The reward of one who directs somebody to do a good deed will be equal to the reward of the latter.

Reported by Muslim

Two Recipes from Raqqa:

1) *Klejay*

This sweet is served during the feast with Arabic coffee.

Ingredients:
- 6 pounds of flour.
- 2 pounds of Arabic butter.
- 3 cups of vegetable oil.
- 1/2 of a cup of milk.
- 2 tablespoons of *mahlab*.
- 2 tablespoons of fennel seeds.
- 2 tablespoons of aniseed.
- 1 tablespoon of yeast.

Method
- Mix the flour, butter and oil until it becomes a solid substance.
- Add some milk to make the dough softer and easy to handle.
- Add the aniseed, fennel seeds, *mahlab* and yeast and knead lightly. Don't wait for it to rise.
- Roll dough into 1/2 inch thickness, and cut into two-inch round circles.
- Place on a greased baking sheet for 8 to 10 minutes or until done.

2) Arabic Coffee

Bitter coffee is most popular beverage in this area. People here say life has no meaning without coffee and it is regarded as the only way to banish sorrow and worry. They also say that if coffee is available, all problems, no matter how great and important, will be easy to solve.
Method:
- Roast the coffee beans and crush them in a mortar to a coarse powder.
- Flavor the powder with cardamom.
- Sometimes saffron or cinnamon are use to flavor it.
- Fresh water is used to make the coffee and no sugar is added.
  This kind of coffee is served in a brass pot that has a long curved spout and is poured into very small cups that have no handles.

Muna Imady

The *Muhafaza* of Hasakeh

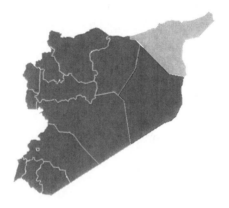

This province lies in the extreme northeast of Syria. It is mainly situated in the Khabour river basin but also extends up to the Tigris river and is one of the largest Syrian provinces. It has witnessed the rise and fall of numerous ancient civilizations such as the Akkadians, the Amorites, the Assyrians, and the Arameans. Among its main archeological sites are: Tell Al Khweira, Tell Halfa, Tell Brak and Tell Hittan.

It is a beautiful province, distinguished by its fertile lands, which are dotted with many water courses and water springs, including some sulphur springs. It is a green land where agriculture has been recently undergone great development, and it is the now the most important source of wheat in the country.

It is also a land of oil production and contains the oil fields of Karactchok, Sweidieh, Rmeilan, Alian and Jabeisseh.

A Folktale from Hasakeh: The Just Qadi

Once upon a time, three wise brothers were traveling in the desert. As they sat down in an oasis to rest, a Bedouin waving a stick approached them.

"I lost my camel just a while ago," he said. "Did you happen to see it in the desert?"

"Was your camel blind in his right eye?" asked the oldest brother.

"Yes," said the Bedouin.

"Was it lame in one foot?" asked the second brother.

"Yes, he was," said the Bedouin.

"Was it missing its tail?" asked the third brother.

"Yes," said the Bedouin.

The oldest brother rubbed his beard and asked, "Was he loaded with wheat on one side and with honey on the other"

"Yes… yes he was!" said the Bedouin. "You must have seen my camel. Tell me where it is!"

"Sorry, we can't help you" said the third brother "We haven't seen your camel!"

"You have stolen my camel!" shouted the Bedouin. "I shall accuse you before the Qadi!"

"Let's go to the Qadi and lay the matter before him," said the oldest brother.

When the four men arrived at the Qadi, they told him their story. The Qadi shook his head thoughtfully then asked the three brothers: "How did you know that the camel had no tail if you had not seen it?"

The oldest brother replied: "When we reached the oasis to rest, we noticed that some of the grass was flattened by some kind of beast. Curiously, the grass blades stood tall, where a tail usually moves from one side to another and pushes down the grass. So we guessed that the animal must have no tail!"

"How did you know the camel was blind in his right eye?" asked the Qadi.

The second brother said: "We knew that because it had eaten grass only on one side of the path while the other remained untouched!"

"How did you know he was lame in one foot?" asked the Qadi.

"We saw the print of one left foot was fainter than the other," said the third brother.

Then the Qadi took a deep breath and asked the brothers: "Now tell me how you could tell what the camel was carrying?"

The oldest brother said: "There were ants on one side and flies on other side. It was obvious that the camel was loaded with wheat on one side and honey on the other!"

The Qadi was greatly pleased with the three brothers' wit and said to the Bedouin, "These brothers have certainly not stolen your camel. Go and search for it and may Allah restore it to you!"

Later on, the Bedouin found his camel wandering near the oasis with its load untouched.

Riddle

I come from water
And I die in water.
What am I? Answer: salt

A Recipe from Hasakeh: Roast Camel

- Kill a camel and remove its skin and its internal organs.
- Wrap the camel in its skin.
- Dig a big hole in the desert and set a large fire and let it burn for a while.
- Put out the fire and lay the camel on the hot embers and smoldering charcoal.
- Cover the camel with hot desert sand for 2-3 hours to allow it to roast.
- Uncover the sand and remove the skin and put the roasted camel on a large tray.
- Serve with rice.
- Best eaten by hand.

Hadith

Anas Bin Malik says that the Holy Prophet (pbuh) said: Allah is pleased with his servant who gives thanks to Him when he he eats and when he drinks.

Reported by Muslim

Glossary

afreet: a male demon or spirit from the Djinn world

al hamdu lillah: thanks be to God.

Allah: God.

boujehayesh: a nickname for jahesh, meaning mule.

duba: a hyena

gouleh: A fabulous female monster from the Djinn world.

hadith: a saying of the Prophet.

hajj: The pilgrimage to Mecca which is one of the five obligations of Islam for all Muslims with the necessary means and health.

hajji: one who performs Hajj

hammam: a public bath.

iqtai: a landowner.

jallekh: a rectangular stone used to sharpen the knives before killing the sheep.

jinn: invisible beings created by God out of fire - they can be good or evil and appear to humans in many disguises.

kan ya ma kan: the traditional beginning of Arab folk-tales - like "once upon a time"

khan: an inn

mahlab: a Syrian spice made from the kernel of the black cherry stone

Mecca: the Holy City of Muslim Pilgrimage in Saudi Arabia

moukhtar: a mayor.

muhafaza: an administrative governorate of Syria

nuss-insais: tiny.

qadi: the judge who settles disputes in an Islamic court of justice.

pbuh: "peace be upon him" - said or written when the Prophet's name is mentioned

soba: a heating stove

tannour: a bread oven made of mud brick.

Tete: Grandma

Umeh: paternal aunt.

wazir: A Minister or a Court Adviser

Syrian Folktales

Other Books by MSI Press

Achieving Native-Like Second-Language Proficiency: Speaking

Achieving Native-Like Second-Language Proficiency: Writing

A Believer-in-Waiting's First Encounter with God

Blest Atheist

Communicate Focus: Teaching Foreign Language on the Basis of the Native Speaker's Communicative Focus

Diagnostic Assessment at the Distinguished-Superior Threshold

El Poder de lo Transpersonal

Forget the Goal: The Journey Counts...71 Jobs Later

How to Improve Your Foreign Language Proficiency Immediately

Individualized Study Plans for Very Advanced Students of Foreign Language

Losing My Voice and Finding Another

Mommy Poisoned Our House Guest

Puertas a la Eternidad

Road to Damascus

Teaching and Learning to Near-Native Levels of Language Proficiency (Vol. 1-4)

Syrian Folktales

Teaching the Whole Class

The Rise and Fall of Muslim Civil Society

Thoughts without a Title

*Understanding the People Around You: An Introduction to
Socionics*

*What Works: Helping Students Reach Native-like
Second-Language Competence*

*When You're Shoved from the Right, Look to the Left:
Metaphors of Islamic Humanism*

Working with Advanced Foreign Language Students

Journal for Distinguished Language Studies (annual issue)

Muna Imady

Syrian Folktales

Muna Imady

CPSIA information can be obtained
at www.ICGtesting.com
Printed in the USA
LVOW10s1434040417
529579LV00010B/687/P